That's What a Friend Is

WRITTEN AND ILLUSTRATED
BY P.K. HALLINAN

 CHILDRENS PRESS, CHICAGO

Library of Congress Cataloging in Publication Data

Hallinan, P   K
  That's what a friend is.

  SUMMARY: Describes friendship in rhymed text and
illustrations.
  [1. Friendship—Fiction. 2. Stories in rhyme]
I. Title
PZ8.3.H15Th   811'.5'4   [E]   76-27744
ISBN 0-516-03628-9

6 7 8 9 10 11 12 R 85 84 83 82

That's What
a Friend Is

A friend is a listener
who'll always
be there

when you've got a big
secret
you just have to share.

A friend is a sidekick
who'll sit by your side

to make you feel better
when you're troubled inside.

And when there's nothing to do on a wet rainy day,

a friend is a pal who'll come over to play.

Friends are just perfect
for all kinds of things,

like walking...

or talking ...

9

or swinging on swings!

And for watching TV,
a friend is the best

for cheering cartoons
with,
and booing the rest.

"

Yes, a friend is the best
one
to hop, skip, or run with...

or just having fun with.

You can sing and shout
'til your tonsils wear out,

'cause that's what having
a friend's all about!

What's a friend for?

For all this,
    and MUCH more!

A friend is a buddy who'll come to your aid

when he thinks you need help,
or you might be afraid.

A friend is a partner who'll stand back to back to protect you from bullies, or an injun attack.

With a friend you can do
what you most like to do!

You can have your own hideouts
in dark, secret places...

or spend the whole day having caterpillar races.

Or just drawing pictures
of each other's faces.

You can laugh...

you can cry...

you can watch cars
go by...

you can have a great time
and not even try!

A friend is a person
who likes to be there....

'cause you two
make a wonderful pair!

And when all's said and done
the natural end is ...

ABOUT THE AUTHOR/ARTIST: Patrick Hallinan first began writing for children at the request of his wife, who asked him to write a book as a Christmas present for their two young sons.

Mr. Hallinan, through his charming text and pictures, shares with all children his delight in the world around him. He lives in southern California.